Farmers Market

Farmers

Carmen Parks

Market

Illustrated by Edward Martinez

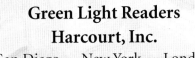

Green Light Readers
Harcourt, Inc.
San Diego   New York   London

www.harcourt.com

First Green Light Readers edition 2002
Green Light Readers is a trademark of Harcourt, Inc.,
registered in the United States of America and/or other jurisdictions.

Library of Congress Cataloging-in-Publication Data
Parks, Carmen.
Farmers market/Carmen Parks; illustrated by Edward Martinez.
p. cm.
"Green Light Readers."
Summary: A girl and her parents spend the day at the farmers' market selling the vegetables they've grown.
[1. Farmers' markets—Fiction.] I. Martinez, Edward, ill. II. Title. III. Series.
PZ7.P2398Far 2002
[E]—dc21 2001002415
ISBN 0-15-216680-7
ISBN 0-15-216674-2 (pb)

A C E G H F D B
A C E G H F D B (pb)

It's still dark, but it's time for me to get up. It's market day in Red Rock.

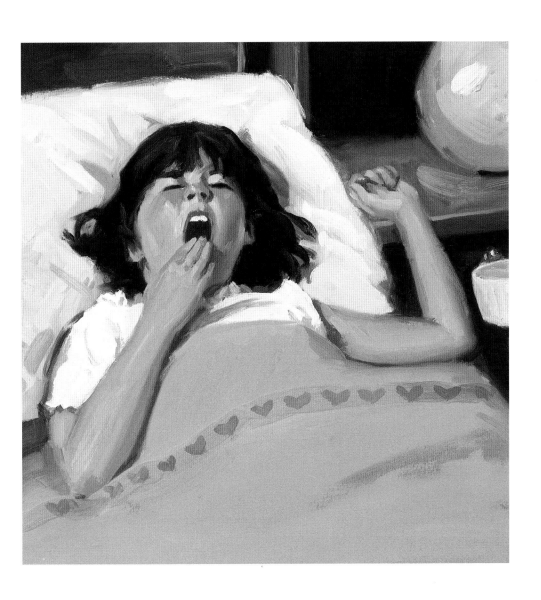

I always go to the market with Mom and Dad. We sell fruits and vegetables from our farm.

We have to get up early because
the market is far away.

As we start out this morning,
the stars are still shining.

At last we get to Red Rock. We park the truck in the big lot and then set up our cart.

We have lots of fruits and vegetables to sell.

"This corn smells fresh," a man says.
"These eggplants look fresh, too."

Lots of people stop at our cart.
My best friend, Carmen, stops by.

Carmen fills her arms with corn.
She gets some lemons, too.

Dad sells the last of the corn.
Now, nothing is left on the cart!

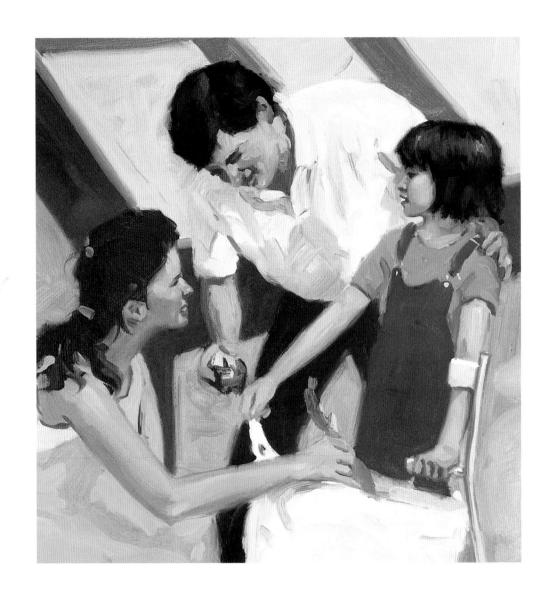

Market day is over. We pick up the trash and go back home.

Market days always go by fast.
I think I like market days the best!

Meet the Illustrator

Edward Martinez loves to paint. He began his work on Farmers Market by taking pictures of real children. Then he looked at the photos as he painted the children in the story. Look closely, the kids might be based on someone you know!

Edward Martinez